Read It, Don't Eat It!

Ian Schoenherr

Greenwillow Books · An Imprint of HarperCollins Publishers

To the bibliothecarians, bibliopolists, and bibliophiles
who have fed me,
with hopes that they can digest this.
And especial thanks to Linda Lapides for the spark,
and to Kathy, Marcia, Virginia, and Paul for the spur.

Read It, Don't Eat It!
Copyright © 2009 by Ian Schoenherr
All rights reserved. Manufactured in China.
www.harpercollinschildrens.com

Permanent ink and acrylic paint on watercolor paper
were used to prepare the full-color art.
The text type is hand lettered.

Library of Congress Cataloging-in-Publication Data

Read it, don't eat it! / by Ian Schoenherr.
p. cm.
"Greenwillow Books."
Summary: Rhyming advice on how to take care of a library book.
ISBN 978-0-06-172455-8 (trade bdg.) — ISBN 978-0-06-172456-5 (lib. bdg.)
[1. Stories in rhyme. 2. Books and reading—Fiction.]
I. Title. II. Title: Read it, do not eat it!
PZ8.3.S3695Re 2009   [E]—dc22   2008027716

First Edition 10 9 8 7 6 5 4 3 2 1

 Greenwillow Books

Read it,
don't eat it.

No dog-ears, please.

Find someplace else to sneeze.

Borrow, don't steal.

TRY not to squeal.

Rips and tears won't magically heal.

Don't overdue it, just renew it.

(Really, now, there's nothing to it.)

Leave no trace
(or at least erase).

Don't censor,
delete, or deface.

It's not a platter,

or a stool.

Be careful with it at the pool.

Don't leave it in the rain or sun.

Please return it
when you're done.

Share with a friend,
a sister, a brother.

Now go out and get another.